OUT OF
STEP

BY JAKE MADDOX

text by
Wendy L. Brandes

STONE ARCH BOOKS
a capstone imprint

Jake Maddox JV Girls books are published by
Stone Arch Books
a Capstone imprint
1710 Roe Crest Drive
North Mankato, Minnesota 56003

www.capstonepub.com

Library of Congress Cataloging-in-Publication Data
Names: Maddox, Jake, author. | Brandes, Wendy L., 1965- author. | Maddox, Jake.
    Jake Maddox JV girls.
Title: Out of step / by Jake Maddox ; text by Wendy L. Brandes.
Description: North Mankato, Minnesota : Stone Arch Books, [2019] | Series: Jake Maddox.
    Jake Maddox JV girls | Summary: Last season Mercy Anderson was one of the best
    dancers on her school's dance team when they almost made it to the state championship,
    but a sudden growth spurt has made her awkward and unsure of her moves. A personal
    coach would help bring her back to competition level, but can she earn enough money dog
    walking to pay for the training?
Identifiers: LCCN 2019008759| ISBN 9781496584694 (hardcover) | ISBN 9781496584717 (pbk.)
    | ISBN 9781496584731 (ebook pdf)
Subjects: LCSH: Dance teams—Juvenile fiction. | Contests—Juvenile fiction. | Growth—
    Juvenile fiction. | Self-confidence—Juvenile fiction. | Money-making projects for
    children—Juvenile fiction. | CYAC: Dance—Fiction. | Dance teams—Fiction. | Contests—
    Fiction. | Growth—Fiction. | Self-confidence—Fiction. | Moneymaking projects—Fiction.
Classification: LCC PZ7.M25643 Oq 2019 | DDC 813.6 [Fic] —dc23
LC record available at https://lccn.loc.gov/2019008759

Designer: Dina Her

Image Credits: Shutterstock: AYakovlev, (dancer) Cover, cluckva, (geometric) design element,
Eky Studio, (stripes) design element, Lucky Business, (feet) back cover, design element,
sergiophoto, (studio) Cover

TABLE OF CONTENTS

CHAPTER 1

TOO TALL?

"Let's practice those moves again," Coach Sara said to the Yardley dance team. "Vine step, then kick, kick, kick, and turn."

Mercy Anderson got ready to go through the routine again. During the past few practices, she had been making more mistakes than usual. *Concentrate,* Mercy thought. *You can do this.*

The music started, and she crossed her left foot over her right. When she followed by crossing her right over her left, she tripped and nearly fell.

Mercy regained her balance and kicked her long legs into the air twice. After the third kick, as she tried to spin, she stumbled again.

Mercy stood up, out of breath and embarrassed.

"That's all for today, girls," Coach Sara said. "We'll get back to it next time."

Mercy walked over to the water fountain, where Lydia Taylor, her best friend, was in line.

"I don't get why I'm having such a hard time with these steps," Mercy said. "We're doing such easy moves."

"You're just having a bad day," Lydia replied. "It happens to everyone."

"I guess," Mercy said. "But I feel like I've been having trouble since we came back from summer break."

"You'll get it back," Lydia said. "Maybe we could do some extra practicing. Your house? Tomorrow?"

"Sounds good!" Mercy said. "Thanks for making me feel better!"

Mercy and Lydia grabbed their dance bags and headed toward the door. As they chatted with their teammates Kyla, Jill, and Ashley, Coach Sara waved them down.

"One more thing, everyone! I forgot to remind you to take measurements for this year's costumes," Coach Sara said. "I need your height, and measure your leg length for tights. Also let me know what size leotard you need. Thanks, girls. See you next time!"

"I hope that this year's costumes are as cool as last year's," Mercy said. "I loved the lilac color with the blue trim."

"Those were so glam," Lydia replied.

"The sequins on the ones we wore for the pop dance were so fun," Jill said.

"I wish those unis still fit," Ashley added.

I've definitely outgrown mine, Mercy thought. *None of my clothes from last year really fit now.*

* * *

Later that night, after dinner, Mercy handed her mom a tape measure. "Can you measure me for my dance-team costume, Mom?" she asked.

"Sure, Merc," Mom said, closing her laptop. "Come into the kitchen. If you stand up against that wall, I can get your height."

Mercy walked toward the wall in the kitchen where her parents had always measured her and her brother, Conor.

Mom pointed to the tallest mark with Mercy's name on it. "This was you almost exactly a year ago," Mom said. "Let's see where you are now."

Mercy stood up against the wall, and Mom made a new mark. After checking the tape measure, Mom grinned. "Mercy, you've grown almost four inches!"

"Really?! That's a lot," Mercy replied. "Can you also measure my legs? Coach Sara wanted those measurements too."

"I'm sure you have a lot more leg to kick nowadays!" Mom said as she measured.

Mercy thought about the issues she'd been having at practice. "Maybe that's my problem," she said. "Maybe I'm just not used to my longer legs. I've been having a harder time doing some moves, like little vine steps and kicks. And the tumbling has been harder for me this year too."

"You know that getting taller changes your center of gravity," Mom responded.

"What do you mean?" Mercy asked.

"When you're smaller, it's sometimes easier to do things like cartwheels and handsprings," Mom said. "As you get taller, the center of your body moves higher, making things a little different."

"So how am I supposed to fix that and get back to dancing the way I used to?" Mercy asked with a frown. "Shrink?"

Mom laughed. "I don't think shrinking is a possibility!" she said. "You could talk to Coach Sara about it. I'm sure a lot of girls have dealt with the same issue."

"I guess," Mercy replied. "Coach Sara is super nice. But sometimes she's hard on girls who can't keep up. She might look at me differently if I told her I was having trouble."

"You'd be surprised, Mercy. I'm sure she'd understand," Mom replied. "In the meantime, you could start doing extra practice to feel more comfortable in your own skin."

"You mean comfortable with my giant body!" Mercy said.

CHAPTER 2

MORE PRACTICE

The next day, Lydia and Mercy hung out in Mercy's yard, playing games and dancing around.

"Listen to this, Mercy," Lydia said, turning up the volume on her phone. A fast song with a strong beat streamed out.

"That's the song we danced to last year in the quad city tournament!" Mercy replied. "I loved that dance, with the back handsprings and the cartwheels."

"Let's try to do all the steps from last year! It'll be fun and good practice," Lydia said.

"I'm up for it," Mercy said. "Restart the song and crank it up."

"Okay, here we go," said Lydia, bouncing her knee. "Five, six, seven, eight."

The girls jumped up to start the dance and then moved easily, twirling and stepping. Halfway through the song, both girls took two giant steps backward. They both did three cartwheels in a row before attempting the back handsprings. Mercy tried to launch herself backward, but she couldn't support her weight and fell to the grass.

"Ugh! I can't seem to do gymnastics moves anymore! I'm all legs!" Mercy said. "I was talking to my mom about it last night. I think I'm having trouble because I grew so much last year."

Lydia switched off the music. "I hadn't even thought about that, but it makes sense," she said. "Let's practice some of the moves that are giving you trouble."

Mercy hopped up. "Okay, sure," she said.

The girls spent the next hour working on cartwheels, roundoffs, walkovers, and handsprings.

"I've never eaten so much dirt!" Mercy said, standing up and dusting her shorts off for what felt like the hundredth time.

"If you keep practicing, you'll get a feel for it," Lydia said. "And I bet Coach Sara would help if you asked."

"My mom said the same thing," Mercy replied. "But remember how she was so tough on Ashley last year when she thought Ashley wasn't paying attention? She didn't even let her dance in the quad city tourney."

"That's because she actually *was* zoning out in practices. This is different," Lydia said. "But if you don't want to talk to Coach Sara, maybe you could work with Coach Kate."

"Who's that?" Mercy asked.

"You know, the outside coach who helped me over the summer," Lydia said, twirling her hair.

"She has really good ideas about everything. She's helped loads of girls."

"Did she help with gymnastics moves?" Mercy asked.

"Yeah, she was great. She gave me a lot of confidence with walkovers, layouts, and handstands," Lydia continued. "I think Coach Kate could really help you."

Mercy got excited for a second and then stopped herself. "I don't think there's any way my family could afford an outside coach," Mercy said, looking down.

She and Lydia never really talked about money, but Mercy had noticed that Lydia always had a lot more spending money than she did.

Lydia gave her a small smile. "Then we'll think about other ways to improve your moves," she said.

"Thanks, Lydia. You are such a great friend," Mercy replied, giving her friend a big hug. "Want to head inside to grab something to eat? My mom baked cookies yesterday."

"Sure!" Lydia replied, walking toward the side door. She stopped for a second and listened. "Do I hear barking?"

Mercy looked toward the street. "You do! There's Ms. Flores with Oscar—the cutest dog ever," Mercy exclaimed. "C'mon, let's go pet him!"

Mercy rushed over to Oscar, a big black Lab. His tail was wagging nonstop. "There's my good boy!" Mercy said, giving the dog a snuggle. She introduced Lydia to both Ms. Flores and Oscar.

"Oscar loves you, Mercy. You're so great with dogs!" Ms. Flores said.

"I wish I had a dog of my own, but at least I can snuggle Oscar once in a while. He's the best doggie around!" Mercy replied. "Seeing him makes me happy!"

"Anytime you want to walk him, come by. Especially in the morning," Ms. Flores said. "I love my dog, but on days when I have early meetings, getting up even earlier to walk Oscar is rough!"

"That definitely sounds tiring!" Mercy replied. "I already have a packed schedule, but anytime I can fit in a walk, I'll let you know."

Oscar gave Mercy one last lick while she petted his back.

"See you later, girls," Ms. Flores said, walking on with Oscar.

"Being with Oscar calms me down," Mercy said. "For the first time today, I stopped worrying about my dancing."

"Maybe some of your mom's cookies will do the same thing," Lydia replied.

Mercy laughed, and the girls raced inside.

CHAPTER 3

DANCE TEAM PLANS

"Gather round, girls," Coach Sara said, clapping. "I just got our schedule. We'll be competing against Chester and Hopewell in our first meet. Then we'll have the big quad city meet three weeks later. The winner of quad city will move on to sectionals."

"Hopewell is G-O-O-D," Kyla whispered loudly enough for her teammates to hear.

"So are we," Jill said.

"What dances are we going to be doing, Coach?" Mercy asked.

"We are going to do two new dance numbers," the coach announced. "A K-pop dance and a hip-hop dance."

"K-pop! That'll be awesome!" Kyla exclaimed.

"And hip-hop is always so fun!" Ashley added.

Mercy gulped. *Those two dances are going to require a lot of tumbling,* she thought.

Coach Sara clapped three times—her way of telling the girls it was time to get to work.

"We're going to incorporate some of what we've been practicing the past few weeks. But most of these dances will be all-new," Coach Sara said. "You're all going to have to push yourselves and work harder than ever."

"We're ready!" Ashley said. The other girls responded with whistles and shouts.

"For the K-pop dance, we're going to do a lot of pairs work," Coach Sara said. "I want you to get into two lines facing each other, and I'll start pairing you up."

Mercy and Lydia shuffled over to the right side of the gym. After scanning the room, Mercy realized that none of the girls was even close to her height. *I'm going to look ridiculous with my partner, whoever she is,* Mercy thought.

"Maybe we'll get paired together, Merc," Lydia said, bumping into Mercy with her shoulder.

"Fingers crossed," Mercy replied. Even if she looked funny with Lydia, at least her bestie wouldn't complain about being paired with a giant.

Coach Sara looked around. "Lydia, you go with Ashley in the front line. Jill, you're with Caroline."

Mercy was relieved that she wasn't with Jill. If anyone was going to complain about being paired with her, Jill was top of the list. It wasn't that Jill was mean, exactly. She just seemed to have an opinion about everything, and often, her opinions were a bit on the snarky side.

"Mercy, you'll be dancing with Kyla. Go to the back line," Coach Sara said.

Mercy looked over at Kyla, who was one of the smaller girls on the team. *I have to stop worrying about being too tall. I'm feeling way too awkward, and I have to get over it!* Mercy thought.

Moving into line next to Mercy, Kyla turned toward her. "It'll be fun to dance with you," Kyla said. "I've always liked how sharp your steps are."

"Thanks, Kyla. I love your energy," Mercy said.

Coach Sara clapped three times and explained the new dance.

"Everybody, listen up. To start, I want your left fist high in the air, then right fist follows, shimmy your shoulders, moving them back and forth quickly, then clap," Coach Sara barked.

The girls did those easy moves with no problem.

"Great job. Now I want you to go down to the floor with your leg folded under you . . . like this," Coach Sara said, demonstrating. "Then jump up and link arms with your partner, circling around each other."

The girls tried going down to the ground. Mercy and Kyla both looked graceful on the way down. But Mercy had a hard time springing up from a seated position. Her right foot seemed to turn to jelly as she tried to get to her feet. *Another thing to work on*, Mercy thought. Mercy and Kyla then circled around and waited for Coach Sara's next instruction.

"We are going to add a little tango and spin," Coach Sara said. "Grab your partners and head to the right with your outside legs and inside legs moving together." She showed the team the steps.

As Coach Sara called out the beats, Mercy and Kyla took an inside step then an outside step. Just as Mercy thought they were getting the hang of it, she tripped over Kyla's legs. Both girls fell to the ground.

Kyla laughed. "This always looks so easy when other people do it," she said.

"Sorry about that. My fault. I think I was zigging when I should have been zagging," Mercy replied, shaking her head.

"We're a pair. We *both* got tangled up. But we'll figure it out," Kyla responded.

After more practice, Coach Sara called, "Girls, you're looking a little tired. Let's take a water break and come back in five.".

As Mercy and Kyla headed to the water fountain, Jill approached them.

"Was it hard for you guys to do the tango?" Jill asked. "I mean with your size difference and all."

From anyone else I would think it was an honest question, Mercy thought. *But with Jill, I'm not so sure.*

"Kyla was a great partner," Mercy said. "On the other hand, I was having a hard time getting into the rhythm."

She waited for a rude reply from Jill, but there wasn't one. Instead Jill nodded. "It's tough learning the steps, especially without the music. Caroline and I were totally out of sync," Jill said.

"I thought it was just me. You know, since I've gotten taller," Mercy said.

"Well, maybe it's that too!" Jill replied, laughing. "I'm just kidding."

"Ha-ha, super funny," Mercy said, annoyed that Jill had gone from supportive to snarky so quickly. Jill just laughed and shrugged her shoulders.

Mercy walked to the other side of the studio and stretched her long legs out on the barre. She knew she couldn't let Jill's comment get to her. She needed to put all her energy toward improving her dance.

Mercy heard the three claps from her coach and walked back onto the floor.

"Before you leave today, girls, I want to review everyone's gymnastics skills," Coach Sara said. "The hip-hop dance will feature a lot of tumbling. So I need to get a sense of where people are."

What if I can't do all the moves Coach Sara wants to see? Mercy worried. *Will I be out of the hip-hop dance? Or off the team?*

Coach Sara pulled a bunch of mats onto the floor. "I want to see cartwheels, a roundoff, a handstand into a walkover, and a back handspring if you can do one," she instructed.

Lydia went first. She was flawless, landing every move perfectly. Kyla and Ashley both looked good too. Then Jill went. Mercy was surprised to see Jill fall over during her handstand. And she didn't have a solid landing on her handspring. That was unusual for her.

Then it was Mercy's turn. She did two perfect cartwheels and a roundoff. Next up, handstand. As she went into her handstand, she knew instantly that she was going to flop. Her legs fell over her head. Mercy tried to pull them in and go into a bridge. That didn't work either.

Ugh! Mercy thought. *Total fail. And now I have to do the back handspring. That's not going to be pretty.*

Mercy went to a spot in the middle of the mat. She took a deep breath and started the move. Jumping backward, she got her hands down, but her arms couldn't support her. She flopped on the mat.

Feeling self-conscious, she pulled herself up and went back into line.

"Don't worry about it, Mercy. You'll get it," Coach Sara said. "You just need to get your timing down."

"I'm working on it, Coach," Mercy said, forcing a smile.

She felt like crying. *It's not just a matter of timing,* she thought. *It's a matter of dealing with a whole new body.*

CHAPTER 4

MAKING A PLAN

Later that day, Mercy pulled up some dance videos on her laptop. She thought that watching skilled, talented dancers would help her.

"Mercy, you've been on the computer for a long time," Mom said, walking into the den. "Why don't you play a game or something with your brother now?"

"I'm watching some dance team videos," Mercy said. "I just want to check out one more. Watch with me, Mom."

"Okay, just one more," Mom said. Mercy started the video.

"Look at that split!" Mom said as the dance reached a big finish. "And that! Did you see how those four girls just did back handsprings at exactly the same time? Wow!"

Mercy smiled. "I know. They're awesome." She shut the laptop and got up from her chair.

Mercy and her mom walked toward the kitchen. "Those girls were so impressive, Mercy," Mom said. "That could be *your* team in a few weeks."

Mercy frowned. "Yeah, but if I don't get it together, I won't be dancing with them," she said. "Coach Sara had us do a gymnastics assessment today. I totally failed."

"What happened?" Mom asked.

"My legs were everywhere," Mercy said. "It's like you said about the 'center of gravity' thing. The bottom half of my body was going one way, and the top half didn't want to help."

Mom chuckled. "I'm sure that some of your teammates are also going through the same thing," she said.

"Nobody has grown as much as I have. I keep messing up, and I feel so awkward," Mercy said. "Maybe I could get some extra help."

"I'm sure that Coach Sara could give you some good pointers," Mom replied.

"Maybe. But I'm afraid that she might just start thinking of me as a weak dancer. She might decide I should sit out until I can get it together," Mercy said. "She's done that with other girls in the past."

"I see what you're worried about," Mom said. "What kind of help were you thinking about, then?"

"Lydia and some of the other girls on the team are getting some private coaching," Mercy replied. "Do you think I could get a lesson or two?"

"I wish we could do something like that for you, Mercy," Mom said, looking at her daughter. "But we don't have money for that right now."

"I didn't think so," Mercy said quickly. "Don't worry, Mom. I understand."

Mom put her hand on Mercy's shoulder. "You'll figure everything out, Mercy. I know you."

"Thanks for believing in me, Mom." Mercy paused. "I just have to believe in myself."

Just then, Mercy's phone rang. It was Lydia. Mercy ran upstairs and answered her call.

"Whatcha doing?" Lydia asked.

"Nothing much. Just watching some dance videos. I still can't believe that I messed up so bad during the gymnastics test," Mercy replied.

"Don't worry about it. You were looking pretty good when we practiced in your yard," Lydia said. "It will all come together. Be patient."

"You're sweet, Lyds. In the meantime, *you* looked great," Mercy said. "You did everything perfectly!"

"It's all because of Coach Kate," Lydia replied. "She helped me with every single move."

"Speaking of Coach Kate, I just talked to my mom.

There's no way I can do outside coaching," Mercy said. "It's just too expensive right now."

"And you don't want to ask Coach Sara for help," Lydia said. "So, let's brainstorm about what else you could do."

After talking for a while, Mercy came up with something.

"I just had an idea," Mercy said. "Maybe I could earn money to pay for private lessons myself. If I babysat or did some dog walking, I might be able to make enough money for one or two sessions with Coach Kate. Do you think that would make a difference?"

"Definitely!" Lydia exclaimed. "I think that's a great idea. Even thirty minutes with Coach Kate would help!"

"I could ask Ms. Flores about walking Oscar in the mornings! Remember? She mentioned it the other day," Mercy replied. "I'm going to run over and talk to her right now. Thanks for your help, Lyds."

After clearing it with her mom, Mercy was out her front door, walking down the street to Ms. Flores' house. Mercy bounded up the front steps and rang the bell. Ms. Flores opened the door, and Oscar ran toward Mercy, wagging his tail.

Mercy bent down and greeted Oscar. "This is the boy I want to see!" Mercy said, hugging the dog.

"Hi, Mercy!" Ms. Flores said. "You're definitely Oscar's favorite neighbor."

Mercy laughed. "And you both are my favorites too!" Mercy said, scratching the dog's neck.

She stood up and looked Ms. Flores in the eye. "Ms. Flores, I'm trying to raise money for some dance coaching," Mercy began. "The other day you said that you could use a hand with morning walks. Do you think I could become your official dog walker?"

"Yes, Mercy, that would be a huge help," Ms. Flores replied. "Like I told you, I have some early-morning meetings, and it's been hard to take care of Oscar and still get out the door on time."

"I'd love to help," Mercy said. "It would be so great to start the day off with Oscar."

"Then let's try it out. Tuesdays, Thursdays, and Fridays. Can you be here at 6:15 a.m.?" Ms. Flores asked.

"That really *is* early!" Mercy said, laughing. "Yes! I can be here. I'll be the best dog walker ever. I promise."

"I know Oscar will be in good hands," Ms. Flores replied, smiling.

"Thank you so much for the chance to do this," Mercy said. "I feel so lucky that I can do something fun and useful to earn money! See you on Tuesday, Oscar!"

CHAPTER 5

TOO TIRED TO TANGO

A few days later, Mercy rushed into the dance studio. She looked around. Only a few girls were there. Mercy plopped down her dance bag, stretched her arms up high, and yawned.

Walking Oscar is tiring! she thought.

Kyla walked in and smiled at Mercy. "I'm glad you're here," she said. "I was hoping we could get some extra time to practice our tango moves."

"Good idea. I'm so happy I made it here with time to spare," Mercy said. "I've been running late ever since I got a new dog-walking job in the mornings."

35

"You walk dogs before school?" Kyla asked. "That must be early!"

"6:15! It's exhausting," Mercy replied. "But I need the money."

"I hope you aren't too tired to tango!" Kyla said, laughing. "Are you ready to work?"

"Yeah! Let's do it!" Mercy agreed.

Mercy and Kyla got into tango position and started dancing down the studio floor. "We're in perfect step," Mercy said, excited that their styles were meshing. "Let's do it again."

This time, Mercy got tripped up on Kyla's foot. Both girls stumbled, but they were able to regain their balance.

"That was on me. I stepped too quickly and ran into you," Mercy said. *I just wish my legs weren't everywhere at once!* she thought.

Jill, who had been standing near Mercy and Kyla when they tripped, walked over. "I don't want to interfere, but Mercy, I think if you take shorter steps, it might be easier for you to keep pace with Kyla," Jill said. "Coach Sara suggested that to me the other day after practice."

Ugh. Thanks for reminding me of how tall and gawky I am, Mercy thought.

"I'll keep that in mind, Jill," Mercy replied.

Before the girls had a chance to try their tango again, Coach Sara came into the room and clapped three times.

"Positions everyone," Coach Sara said. "We'll start with the K-pop dance."

Three more claps and the girls were in line, ready to go. Coach Sara turned on the music.

Mercy went through the moves in her head as she danced. *Right fist, left fist, shimmy then clap. Spin around your partner.*

"Mercy, you have it backward," Coach Sara said, stopping the routine. "It's left fist, then right fist. Let's do it again."

Mercy was so tired she struggled to pay attention.

Still, everything was going well until the girls set up for cancan kicks. Mercy was a second slow on the first kick and then rushed herself to catch up.

I'm slower because my long legs take longer to get up in the air, Mercy thought. She had to make adjustments to correct the mistake for good. She couldn't let that happen during a performance.

The girls then broke the circle and went into their two lines. It was tango time.

Mercy and Kyla followed behind Jill and Caroline, who were to their right. They tangoed for ten steps, and then Coach Sara stopped the music again.

"Okay, ladies, we are going to add a little spice to the tango. You will tango down on one side and then, on your return, you will grab your partner's hand," Coach Sara said, demonstrating. "Make an arch with your arms, and one of you will twirl under. Then the other one will do the same. Each partner will continue twirling until you're both back where you started."

Mercy gulped. *How's that going to work?* she wondered. *I'm so much taller than Kyla. It's going to look weird when I go under.*

The girls got into formation and tried out the new steps. Kyla and Mercy made an arch with their arms. Kyla ducked under and then went onto her toes to hold her arm up for Mercy to duck under. Mercy slouched as she passed through. Then Kyla took her turn, and then Mercy again.

"Stop! I'm not sure that's going to work," Coach Sara said.

Good! I'm not so sure either, Mercy thought.

"I didn't realize that there was such a big height difference between Mercy and Kyla!" Coach Sara said. "Mercy has to slouch *way* down to go under the bridge."

Mercy wanted to slink off the dance floor. *Totally embarrassing,* Mercy thought. *First I messed up on simple steps, now the whole team has to do a new combo because I'm a total ostrich. Argh!*

"What we'll do instead is have the taller girl of the pair raise her arm up and the smaller one will go under and twirl," Coach Sara said, revising the dance. "The tall girl will take two steps forward and the smaller girl will twirl again."

Feeling down on herself, Mercy didn't pay close attention when they redid their dance steps. As Kyla twirled, Mercy stepped and they collided. It was the third time today that Mercy had made a wrong step.

Maybe I'm having extra trouble because I'm so exhausted from dog walking, Mercy thought.

But she had to keep at it. The only way she was going to be able to deal with her new center of gravity was by getting extra help. And lessons with Coach Kate wouldn't pay for themselves.

CHAPTER 6

EXTRA SLEEP

Two days later, Mercy was back to early-morning dog walking. She almost overslept, hitting the snooze button on her alarm one too many times. After bolting out of bed, Mercy rushed around, got dressed, wolfed down her breakfast, and stuffed her books into her backpack. Within ten minutes she was out the door and headed over to pick up Oscar.

After today's morning walk, I'll only need about four more walks to pay for a session with Coach Kate, Mercy thought.

As Mercy neared Ms. Flores' house, she realized that she had forgotten to pack her dance bag and would have to stop at home after walking Oscar. She had too much to think about!

Mercy let herself in to Ms. Flores' house, hugged Oscar, and grabbed his leash. She was about to head out when Ms. Flores greeted her from the kitchen.

"Hi, Mercy! How are you? You've been doing a great job with Oscar. I can't thank you enough!" Ms. Flores said. "Is there any chance that you could take him for his dinner walk this evening too?"

"I have dance practice until 6:00," Mercy replied.

"He can wait until about 6:30," Ms. Flores said. "It would really help me out."

Mercy thought about the extra money she'd earn. She'd be that much closer to her private lesson. "If I rush back from dance, I could maybe get here in time," Mercy said slowly.

"Great! Then you and Oscar have a date! Thanks so much!" Ms. Flores said.

I hope I'm not overdoing it, Mercy thought, but she quickly shook off the thought. *I'll be okay if I just stay focused.*

* * *

After a long day at school, Mercy was back at practice. She was trying to keep up but was having a hard time staying awake.

"Okay, ladies," Coach Sara said to the group. "I like the way the K-pop dance is shaping up. I think we've got something good going. But since our first competition is in two weeks, we have to get going on the hip-hop dance. Are you ready to learn the steps?"

The girls were pumped. "I hope we get to do some gymnastics," Ashley said.

"You won't be disappointed!" Coach Sara replied, with a grin.

She arranged the girls into three lines, resembling a loose pyramid. Mercy was in the back line, next to Lydia on one side and Jill on the other.

Coach Sara clapped three times. "On a three count, I want each of you in the back line of our pyramid to bounce down to the floor in a jazz split. Then everybody will bounce back up. The two girls on each side of a middle girl will lift her up and send her into a flip with a kick-over."

That should be no problem. Except getting out of the split, Mercy thought.

One, two, three. Mercy, Lydia, and Jill jumped into the split. They all popped up, and on another count of three, Lydia rested on Jill's and Mercy's shoulders and went into a nice kick-over.

"Good job, Lydia," said Mercy.

"Now the girl on the left will move into the middle. The other two will support her, and she will do the same thing that the first girl just did," Coach Sara said.

Jill moved into the middle. Lydia and Mercy lifted her. Jill's kick-over was a little shaky. She finished off to the side.

"Now the girl on the right will move to the middle. You know the drill!" Coach Sara shouted.

Lydia and Jill had a hard time supporting Mercy. And Mercy, who felt as if Jill and Lydia were sagging, rushed her kick-over. Like Jill, she landed off to the side. Totally shaky.

"That was rough," Jill said.

"I'll say," Mercy agreed, trying to be a good sport. "But we don't have time to worry about it. Coach is already moving on to different stuff."

Coach Sara showed the girls some high knees and had them drop to the ground into a plank position, then jump up and turn in a pirouette. The girls were all learning the steps slowly, but there were no major spills.

Just as Mercy started to get some confidence, Coach Sara yelled, "Take a five-minute break, and we'll go on to the big finish."

Mercy grabbed her water bottle and sat on a mat on the ground. *I'm glad to have a break,* she thought.

I'm so tired I could curl up in a ball and go to sleep right here. The dog walking is definitely catching up to me.

Mercy leaned back against the wall and closed her eyes for a second. The next thing Mercy knew, Lydia was squatting down next to her.

"Merc, wake up. You must have dozed off for a second," Lydia whispered, tapping Mercy's shoulder. "You've got to get up. Coach Sara is getting ready to teach us the big finish."

Mercy turned her head. "I'm so tired, Lyds," Mercy said. "Dog walking has just wiped me out."

"C'mon, get up and move around," Lydia said, pulling Mercy up from the mat. "Remember, you're dog walking to raise money to become better at dancing. You can't let Oscar sink your dance career!"

Mercy laughed and stretched. "I'm ready," she said, suppressing a yawn.

Coach Sara clapped three times. "Break's over, girls! Back to work!" she said. "Now for the start of the big finish. I want all of you girls in the back row to go into a long handstand, move into a walkover, spring up, drop to the floor in plank position, and then jump up for the very end."

"OMG. That's going to be rough!" Mercy said. *Especially since I just woke up!* she thought.

"I know!" Ashley said.

"We can do this!" Jill said.

"Into the handstand on my count," Coach Sara shouted. "Then hold for five." She counted off and the girls hit their handstands.

One, two, three, four, five. Mercy was able to pull herself into a handstand, but she couldn't hold it through Coach Sara's long count. She tipped over into a backbend without meaning to. From the floor she saw Ashley flop over as well.

"Argh," Mercy exclaimed.

"Not to worry, back row!" Coach Sara yelled. "Let's try it again!"

This time, Mercy held her handstand for a little longer, but still not as long as they were supposed to.

I'm just not good at this, she thought. *Maybe I should just give up on the hip-hop dance!*

"You'll all get there," Coach Sara said. "Let's do it again. This time, we'll hold the handstand for a little less time. That might make it easier."

Mercy, along with all the girls in the back row, was able to hold the handstand through a count of three. Then they went into the walkover. Mercy walked her legs over, but she couldn't pop up from the bridge and collapsed onto the floor.

This is so frustrating, Mercy thought.

They practiced a few more times. At one point, Mercy hopped up and circled to the right, when she should have gone left.

"Mercy!" Coach Sara shouted, "You went the wrong way! You have to pay attention! And let's see some more pep in your step!"

"Sorry, Coach!" Mercy replied, super embarrassed. She spent the rest of practice trying to look a lot more peppy than she felt.

Finally Coach Sarah ended practice. "We're going to wrap up for today," she said. "I thought that you were all off to a good start. We'll keep practicing and nail it down! Great job today, girls." She clapped three times and practice was over.

The girls gathered their things. "We're never going to make it to the sectionals if we don't start stepping it up," Jill mumbled as she zipped up her bag.

"This was just our first day practicing this dance," Mercy said. "We'll all pick up the steps."

"We have to!" Jill replied. "We have almost no time before our first competition. If we are going to get a good score on the hip-hop dance, we have to get a lot better fast! I'm going to see if Coach Sara can stay for some extra help."

I wonder how that will go. I'm surprised that Jill isn't worried about Coach Sara benching her, Mercy thought.

She looked at the clock on the wall. She was so tired. Rushing to walk Oscar was the last thing she wanted to do, but she had to stick to the plan.

CHAPTER 7

COACH KATE

After another long week of school, practice, and dog walking, Mercy was exhausted. But with a few extra evening walks, she had finally raised enough money to schedule a private lesson. Dog walking might have zapped her energy for practice, but Mercy was sure her lesson with Coach Kate would totally be worth it.

"I can't believe that I'm *finally* going to meet Coach Kate," Mercy said into her phone as she walked to the rec center.

"You have done miles and miles of dog walking to make it happen!" Lydia replied on the other end.

"It's been fun, but so tiring. Getting up at six a.m. is rough!" Mercy said.

"But you must feel really good about paying for your own session," Lydia said.

Mercy couldn't help but smile. She *was* proud of herself. "Hopefully, it helps," Mercy replied.

"You've been doing great lately," Lydia said. "Your tango is looking good."

"Thanks, Lydia, but I'm still worried. My moves for the hip-hop dance are off. My center of gravity is too high, and my energy level is too low!" Mercy said.

"That's why you're going to work with Coach Kate!" Lydia reminded her. "Try to have a positive attitude."

"You're sure that Coach Kate can help me with my handstand and my walkover?"

"Yes, she can help. Hopefully, one session is enough," Lydia said. "Call me when you're done."

"Definitely!" Mercy said, clicking off her phone.

Mercy arrived at the rec center and waited for Coach Kate to show up. After a few minutes, a very tall, athletic-looking woman walked in. She looked around and then spotted Mercy. "I'm Coach Kate. Are you Mercy?" she asked.

"Yes, I am. Nice to meet you!" Mercy replied.

"Tell me what you are having trouble with, Mercy," Coach Kate said, getting right down to business.

"Like I told you on the phone, I've grown a lot over the past six months. I feel like I'm constantly tripping all over myself," Mercy explained.

Coach Kate smiled. "You remind me of myself," she said.

"Really?" Mercy responded.

"I had a wicked growth spurt when I was a little older than you. It took me a while to figure out how to dance with my new long legs," Coach Kate said. "I want to be honest with you, it was *a ton* of work."

Mercy frowned. "I figured," she said. Things were not getting off to a promising start.

"I don't mean to discourage you, Mercy," Coach Kate said. "I'm sure you'll get there. Why don't you warm up your muscles, and then we'll start to work on your problem areas."

After Mercy stretched and did some warm-up steps, she was ready.

"Where do you want to start?" Coach Kate asked.

Mercy went through the K-pop dance and the hip-hop dance in her mind. "I'm having a hard time holding a handstand and doing front walkovers," she said.

"Let's work on handstands first," Coach Kate said. She asked Mercy to get up into a handstand, resting her legs on the wall.

My arms feel like noodles, Mercy thought as she went into the move.

Just as Coach Kate told Mercy to move her hands away from the wall, Mercy fell out of the handstand.

"Sorry, Coach. Let me get back up into the handstand," Mercy said.

"No worries, Mercy. Let's try again," Coach Kate replied.

Mercy kicked her legs up and tried to follow Coach Kate's instructions. She moved along the wall with her hands, but then she had to reset herself again.

Mercy stood up. "I'm having a really hard time all the way around," she said.

"I noticed your legs were drooping," Coach Kate responded. "Are you tired?"

Mercy was surprised by the question. *Of course I'm tired,* she thought. *I've been getting up super early. Plus, on days when I've walked Oscar at dinnertime, I've been up late doing homework.*

"My schedule has been a little rough lately. I guess I'm more exhausted than I thought," Mercy admitted.

"Do you want to reschedule? I have some time next week," Coach Kate said. "I want you to get as much as you can out of this lesson."

Mercy though it was generous of Coach Kate to offer to reschedule. But she knew if she waited another week, she wouldn't be ready for the first dance competition.

"Maybe we could just try again?" she asked.

"Let's continue, then," Coach Kate said. She asked Mercy to try to get into a bridge position.

"But we aren't doing back walkovers in our dance," Mercy said.

"Learning all of these moves is a process, Mercy," Coach Kate said. "Getting into a bridge, you feel your center of gravity. That will help you with your other moves."

"That sounds good, but I don't know if I have time for a process," Mercy said. She was starting to worry that one lesson wouldn't be enough.

"Let's try it to see if that helps you figure things out," Coach Kate said.

Throughout the lesson, Coach Kate gave Mercy some tips, but it wasn't the big fix that Mercy thought it would be. Mercy worried that the lesson didn't help enough. She doubted that she would be ready for the tumbling section of the hip-hop dance. And she was scared that she'd ruin her team's chances of winning.

CHAPTER 8

HOPEWELL FACE-OFF

The following week, Mercy's parents drove her to the dance studio. The girls were going to take a bus to Hopewell for the first tournament.

"How do you think the team will do today?" Dad asked.

"I'm kind of worried," Mercy said. "You know I've been having trouble with the tumbling in the hip-hop dance—even after my session with Coach Kate."

"But you've put in so much hard work," Mom said as the car came to a stop. "I'm sure that all of your effort will pay off. Good luck today, sweetie!"

"Thanks, Mom," Mercy replied. "And thanks for driving me!"

She hopped out of the car and walked toward the members of the Yardley team who were already gathered in front of the dance studio.

Mercy set her dance bag down and joined Jill, Ashley, and Kyla, who were all jumping up and down and limbering up.

"Hey, Mercy!" Ashley said. "We were just talking about the hip-hop dance."

Mercy wished she felt more confident. She had been so sure that Coach Kate was going to fix all her issues, but she didn't feel as if she had made *any* progress. "I have my fingers crossed," Mercy said. If only they'd had another week or two to practice.

The rest of the team arrived, and the girls filed onto the bus to go to Hopewell.

Coach Sara played upbeat music as they rode to the competition. The girls were pumped up by the time they arrived at the Hopewell gym. They walked onto the gym floor, where the Hopewell and Chester teams were already warming up.

Yardley was first up with the K-pop dance. They took the stage, and Mercy shook out her arms and legs, getting ready. She was so nervous. *I hope that I don't mess up the tango!* she thought.

Kyla stood behind Mercy as they got ready to file onto the dance floor. "Mercy, we've got this. You look awesome when we tango. The judges are going to love it!" Kyla exclaimed.

The girls walked onto the floor and took their positions in two lines. Mercy fist-bumped Kyla on one side and Ashley on the other.

The music started and they were off—left fist, right fist, shimmy, clap. *The first tough move is coming up,* Mercy thought. Down to the floor, pop up, and spin around. The girls looked great. The dance continued, and it was time for the tango.

Their tango was crisp. On the way back, Kyla gracefully twirled under their arms. Perfect!

The last piece was the cancan kicks. Mercy was a beat late getting into position and then was out of step with her three kicks. And it only got worse from there!

As she rushed to get back into time, Mercy lost her focus and circled to the left instead of the right. She fell completely out of sync.

Her mistake was probably going to cost the team a good score in the dance. She might have even lost them the entire competition.

After they took their bows, Mercy rushed off the stage. She'd completely blown it. How could she face her teammates?

Coach Sara caught up to her. She put her hand on Mercy's shoulder. "Mercy, what happened out there?" Coach Sara asked quietly.

Mercy sniffed, trying to hold back tears.

"You haven't been yourself these past few weeks. You've been dragging. And it seems like it's been hard for you to concentrate," Coach Sara said. "Tell me what's going on with you."

Mercy shrugged and wiped her eyes, which were overflowing. She decided to come clean. "I'd been feeling kind of shaky since the season started," she said. "When you asked for our measurements, I realized that my growth spurt must have been affecting my dancing. I grew four inches, and I guess I haven't figured out how to dance with my new height."

"I wish you had talked to me about that. Rapid growth can definitely affect your dancing temporarily, but it's something we can work through," Coach Sara said softly. "I'm seeing something else, though. Like you're sleeping through practices. Forgetting dance moves."

Mercy's face flushed. "I've just been so tired." She took a breath and looked at her coach. "I thought that if I asked you for extra help, you might think that I was hopeless. So I got a dog-walking job to help pay for a lesson with an outside coach," Mercy explained. "Now I'm realizing that the dog walking was wearing me out."

"Oh, Mercy. It sounds like you were giving it your all. But you should know that you can always come to me and your teammates for help," Coach Sara said. "That's what being on a team is all about. Going forward, we can figure this out together."

"Thanks for being so understanding, Coach," Mercy said. "I'm so sorry about my mistakes in the dance."

Coach Sara gave Mercy's shoulder a squeeze. "Keep your head up. We all make mistakes, Mercy," she said. "Do you feel like you are up for dancing in the hip-hop dance?"

Mercy looked down, taking a moment to think. Finally she spoke. "After my big mistake just now, and everything else, I think I should bench myself," she said, keeping her eyes on the floor. "I'm having a hard time with the gymnastics and some of the dance steps. I think it would be better for the team if they went on without me." She glanced up at her coach.

Coach Sara nodded. "No worries. I can show Jill

and Lydia how they can fill your spot on the dance floor," she said. "I know you're disappointed, Mercy, but I'm proud of you for putting the team first. You are one of the most dedicated dancers on the team. We will go forward and work on your challenges together. I promise."

* * *

Mercy watched from the sidelines as her team competed in the hip-hop dance without her. Jill and Lydia did back walkovers into splits instead of doing the kick-overs. *I wish I was out there with them, but I made the right decision*, she thought.

Yardley's dance wasn't perfect, but it was solid. Mercy cheered on her teammates as they took their bows. She ran up to Kyla, Lydia, Jill, and Ashley after they finished, congratulating them.

"Thanks, Mercy!" Kyla said. "You'll get it back. And we'll be stronger with you in the mix."

"I agree!" Jill said, hugging Mercy.

The loudspeaker crackled, and the girls held each other tight in a circle. The chief judge's voice boomed, "Yardley received a ninety-two in its hip-hop dance."

The girls jumped around—they had guaranteed themselves at least second place. Mercy tried to act excited, but she was disappointed in herself.

I didn't contribute to this performance at all. I'm not letting that happen again, she thought. *I'm going to be solid for the quad city tournament.*

CHAPTER 9

GETTING READY

On the bus ride home from Hopewell, Coach Sara sat down next to Mercy. "This week and next, I'd love it if you would do some extra practices with me," she offered.

"That's really generous of you, Coach," Mercy said. "There's nothing that I'd like more than to work hard and fix my issues."

"I know, Mercy, and we can get you on the right track before the quad city tourney," Coach Sara said. "So, extra practice starts tomorrow."

"I'll be ready!" Mercy exclaimed. "I'm excited to have a fresh start."

Mercy and Lydia got off the bus together and walked toward Mercy's mom, who was waiting to drive them home.

"How are you doing, Merc?" Lydia asked.

"I'm disappointed I didn't realize that I was making everything harder by wearing myself out," Mercy said.

"I feel like I'm to blame," Lydia replied. "I kept telling you that Coach Kate would fix everything."

"It isn't your fault. Maybe if I had a week or two to work with Coach Kate, she could have helped me more," Mercy said. "I should have talked to Coach Sara. Both you and my mom tried to tell me that Coach Sara would help me."

"No more dog walking?" Lydia asked.

"With Coach Sara's help, I won't need to earn extra money. I can get some more sleep! I can still walk Oscar in the evenings if I have time," Mercy said.

"It seems like you have a good plan," Lydia said. "I know you'll be ready for the quad city tourney."

* * *

After the next practice, Mercy was excited to put in some extra work with Coach Sara. Mercy was surprised to see Jill staying late as well.

"Coach Sara said that you'd be joining us for extra help," Jill said. "I broke my wrist this summer, and tumbling has been so much harder for me this season. Coach Sara has helped me get my strength and timing back."

"I had no idea that you had hurt yourself," Mercy said. "How are you feeling now?"

"Much better these past two weeks," Jill replied. "Coach Sara was really supportive."

"Wow. I didn't know that you were having problems," Mercy said. "I'm having trouble too. It's harder for me to hold a handstand and do a walkover now that I've grown so much."

"I'm surprised, Mercy. You've always been one of our best dancers," Jill said. She swallowed hard. "Did I make you feel bad when I commented on your height? I was just kidding around."

Mercy shrugged. "I don't think anyone *meant* to make me feel funny about being tall."

"I'm sorry if I made you feel bad. I think you look awesome," Jill said. "I wish my legs were long like yours."

Mercy smiled. "Thanks, Jill. That means a lot," she replied. "I think we could really help each other."

"I'd be down for that. I'd do anything that would get us past Hopewell!" Jill responded.

Coach Sara walked over. "I'm excited to have the chance to do some extra work with the two of you at once!" she said. "First, we'll work on holding the handstands. Then, once we've mastered that, we'll move on to the front walkover."

Both girls lined up and went into handstands against the wall. After that, Coach Sara had the girls lean over a bench and pull their torsos up with their arms.

"That was really helpful," Mercy said. "I'm starting to figure out how to control my gigantic legs!"

Jill smiled.

They moved on to working on the front walkover. Coach Sara worked with them individually to make sure that they each felt comfortable doing the move.

"Is your wrist hurting?" Mercy asked.

"I'm doing pretty well," Jill answered. "Your long legs look great on your handstands."

This time, Mercy knew that Jill was being supportive. "Thanks!" Mercy said. "I'm starting to believe that we can pull everything together before the quad city tournament."

* * *

A week later, the entire team was in the dance studio, practicing hard for the upcoming quad city tournament. As they were running through their

K-pop dance, Coach Sara stopped the music right before the team got to the tango.

"Mercy and Kyla, I want to see how you two look in front. Come forward," Coach Sara said. "At our last meet, one of the judges mentioned that they like to see girls of different sizes doing everything in sync. I think it might help us get a higher score on the K-pop dance if you girls are in front."

I can't believe it! Coach Sarah trusts us to be front and center—that's huge! Especially after my big mistake in competition, Mercy thought. *I just hope I don't mess up and disappoint her.*

"We'll take it from the top," Coach Sara said. She started the music, and the girls did everything smoothly right up to the tango. After Kyla and Mercy tangoed down the floor, Coach Sara said, "I liked the way that looked, girls. We'll keep the lines like this for now."

Mercy and Kyla were super excited that Coach Sara was confident in their dancing.

Everyone had gotten more comfortable with the hip-hop dance. Even if they weren't perfectly in sync, they were very close. Coach Sara had also cut down the time for holding the handstand, which made it easier for everyone in the back row to go into the walkover.

"We're definitely stronger with this part of the dance," Mercy said to Lydia and Jill after they each did their handstands and walkovers.

"The extra sessions with Coach Sara really helped," Jill said. "I think we're all in a groove."

"Agreed," Lydia chimed in.

Mercy smiled. "We're ready to go out and take the championship from Hopewell!"

CHAPTER 10

QUAD CITY TOURNAMENT

One week later, the girls traveled to the quad city tournament at Franklin Hills. Four teams were competing—Franklin Hills, Hopewell, Garden City, and Yardley.

Just like the year before, the gym was completely filled with spectators. As they walked around, Mercy scanned the crowd. *There are so many people. How am I going to find my family?* she thought.

Looking up high in the bleachers, she saw a big sign on bright yellow poster board that said *We Heart Mercy* with a big picture of a black dog on it.

Conor was holding the sign. He was standing next to her parents *and* Ms. Flores! *They all came! That's so sweet!* Mercy thought. She was determined to dance her best for all of them—even Oscar!

The Yardley squad was going to be the third team to dance the K-pop dance. They were going to follow Garden City and Franklin Hills.

Coach Sara took the girls into a separate area of the gym. They did a quick run-through of both dances.

"You girls can do this," Coach Sara said when they'd finished. "We've had a few more weeks to practice, and now you're ready! You girls will knock their socks off with your crisp steps in the K-pop dance and with the big finish in hip-hop."

The girls were too amped up to watch the other teams dance. Instead they stretched and fidgeted.

Garden City went first. Their music played—they danced to a pop song that the Yardley team had done a routine to last season. While the music played,

Mercy and her teammates fooled around, doing some of their old moves.

Toward the end of the song, they heard a burst of applause. "I forgot that the fans were so loud at this tournament," Mercy said.

"I bet our old dance was better," Ashley said. "We'd be getting twice as much applause!"

The girls laughed and continued dancing around.

When the music stopped, they listened for the score. Over the loudspeaker they finally heard, "Garden City receives an eighty-six in the pop dance."

"Eighty-six is beatable," Jill said.

"We scored better than that in our last meet," Mercy said. *And that was after I totally messed up,* she thought.

"Maybe the judges are super tough," Kyla added.

"We should just be thinking about our own dance," Mercy said.

About ten minutes later, the Franklin Hills team was announced. They were dancing to this past summer's hottest song. As the Franklin Hills team danced, there were three bursts of applause and lots of cheering from the crowd.

"Ugh," Lydia said. "Their fans are so loud!"

"Don't worry. Ours will be louder," Jill replied.

Once Franklin Hills' dance finished, Coach Sara clapped three times to get her team's attention. "We're up next. Put your game faces on. Don't pay attention to anything besides your teammates and the music," Coach Sara said.

Mercy stretched and Coach Sara walked over.

"You look really good with your long legs, Mercy," Coach Sara said.

"I finally feel good about being tall and owning the dance," Mercy replied. "It's thanks to you, Coach."

"You're the one who put in the work, Mercy," said Coach Sara.

"I know that I'm ready this time," Mercy said, smiling. After weeks of worrying, Mercy finally felt like her old self again. Maybe even better than before.

The girls walked to the other side of the gym. As they headed toward the stage, they saw the Franklin Hills team huddled together, waiting for their score.

Filing out onto the main gym floor, they heard, "Franklin Hills earns a ninety-four on the pop dance."

"That's a high score," Mercy said to Lydia.

"We can do better than that," Lydia replied. "We've changed things up since our last competition. You and Kyla are front and center now. The judges will notice those long, graceful legs."

"Gulp," Mercy said. "I had almost forgotten that we were going to be center stage."

"You and Kyla have been great in practice this week," Lydia said. "Plus you've put in a ton of extra work. We're ready."

Mercy nodded, suddenly feeling the pressure. *Take a breath,* she thought. *You're ready.*

"Look," Kyla pointed to the crowd. "Mercy, isn't that your brother over there with the sign?"

"Yeah, isn't the sign cute?" Mercy said.

"I bet the black dog is supposed to be Oscar," Lydia commented.

Seeing Ms. Flores and the drawing of Oscar made Mercy even more determined to nail down her performance. *I put in so much hard work to get here,* Mercy thought. *Let's do this.*

The music started and the girls went into their routine. They had practiced it so many times that it felt completely familiar and automatic.

Mercy tried to stay in the moment, thinking only about the move that she was doing. Not getting ahead of the dance.

Time for the tango, Mercy thought. *Relax and stand tall!*

Inside foot, outside foot, inside foot, outside foot. There was a giant cheer. *Block it out,* Mercy said to herself.

They headed back toward the center of the stage. Kyla twirled, and as she was getting ready to take a step, her foot skidded. Mercy was still holding Kyla's hand up high. She grabbed tighter and Kyla regained her balance. Mercy hoped the mistep went unnoticed.

Next came the cancan. *I have to make sure I'm in time with my kicks,* Mercy thought.

Three kicks and a few turns later, the music ended and the crowd whooped.

The girls took a bow and then showed their appreciation to the crowd by clapping their hands up high. They filed off the gym floor and began high-fiving each other.

"We did it!" Jill shouted.

"Everyone was so awesome!" Mercy yelled, giving Jill a huge hug.

They huddled up and did a Yardley cheer. As they waited for their score, Kyla said, "You saved me, Mercy. If you hadn't pulled me along during our last dance run, I would have slipped. I took a bad step and you fixed it."

Mercy grinned. "Like you always say, we make a good team," she said.

After what seemed like forever, the judges announced the score. "Yardley received a ninety-six on the pop dance."

The girls went crazy, jumping up and down and fist-bumping.

Three claps from Coach Sara and the celebration stopped. Coach Sara gathered the girls close to her. "I'm so very proud of you all. You did it. But our work isn't done," Coach Sara continued. "We have another dance to do."

"What's our schedule? When do we do the hip-hop dance?" Ashley asked.

"Hopewell will dance. We'll have a break. And then we'll dance according to what place we're in. If we're in second place, we dance second to last. If we are in first place, we'll dance last."

"Then let's hope we dance last!" Mercy said.

CHAPTER 11

LAST DANCE

At the end of the first round, Yardley was in first place. Hopewell was one point behind, while Franklin Hills trailed by two. Garden City was ten points down.

No one is going to make this easy for us, Mercy thought. *If we're going to win, we're going to have to go out there and earn it.*

As the second round heated up, the girls got more and more anxious.

"I wish we could have gone first," Jill said.

"All this waiting around is making me edgy," Mercy agreed.

The afternoon seemed to drag on. Just like in the first round, the girls decided not to watch their competition. They hung around a different part of the huge gym, which was separated by a curtain. Every once in a while, though, one of the girls would take a peek and report back about what the other teams were doing.

After Garden City finished its dance, the girls got a little more nervous and hyper. They tried not to listen as the scores were reported. But after Franklin Hills finished up, Ashley bolted into the other part of the gym and looked up at the scoreboard.

"Franklin Hills scored a ninety-five this round," Ashley said, breathlessly. "Hopewell is on next, and then we're up."

"So if Franklin Hills scored a ninety-five, that means that if we get a ninety-four or above, we beat them," Mercy said, calculating their chances.

"But Hopewell still has to go. And you know they're going to go all out and bring it," Kyla said.

Hearing that makes me nervous! Mercy thought. Then she shoved the thought away. The hip-hop dance could still be rough, but she felt so much more confident in her dancing thanks to Coach Sarah—and her own hard work.

"Back row, let's practice some handstands," Jill said to the group. "You know, instead of just standing around."

"Good idea," Lydia said.

Mercy, Jill, Lydia, and Ashley walked over to the gym wall and went up into handstands. Mercy supported her weight with no problem. She knew she would hit the handstands at the end of her dance.

"Mercy, we've both got this," Jill said.

"Absolutely. We are ready," Mercy said, feeling confident.

"The Hopewell girls have finished," Ashley said. "Coach wants us all together."

Coach Sara walked over to her team. "Okay, everyone, this is the moment we've worked for," she said. "Just give it your all. If you give everything you've got, then you're winners, no matter what the score says. Just trust each other."

"Hands in," Mercy called.

The girls huddled up, put their hands in, and cheered, "Yardley!"

They filed to the center of the gym floor and took their spots.

Don't be nervous, Mercy thought. *Just give it your all, like Coach Sara said.*

The music started. Everything was going well. Planks, cartwheels, roundoffs. Everyone was hitting their spots and dancing with high energy.

It was the last few moves that were going to win it or lose it for the team. They went into their pyramid formation. Their first big trick went well—Lydia did her kick-over perfectly. Jill and Mercy weren't quite as perfect, but they were both solid on the landing.

First part done! Mercy thought. *I just have to focus on the final moves and it'll all be okay.*

After a count of four, the girls in the back row went into their handstands. They all held the move for the full count, split their legs, and went into the walkover.

I did it! I did it! Mercy thought as she jumped up from her walkover. She heard the crowd cheering loudly and broke into a big smile.

She quickly refocused on going into the plank and jumping up. Dance over!

Mercy looked around at her teammates, then the stands. The crowd was going crazy. She saw her family and Ms. Flores standing and clapping. The girls took their bows and ran out to the other side of the gym to wait for their scores.

Coach Sara met them as they came off the stage. "Well done, girls. Well done!" Coach Sara said. "You should be incredibly proud of yourselves! The hip-hop dance was a huge success!"

The girls jumped up and down and clapped.

"Coach Sara," Ashley said. "How much do we need to score to beat Hopewell?"

Coach Sara frowned slightly. "They pulled a ninety-six," she said. "We'd have to get a ninety-seven or above to win it outright. Ninety-six gives us a tie."

The girls got quiet.

"Do we have a chance, Coach?" Mercy asked quietly.

"Of course," Coach Sara said. "But whatever your score is, you girls have done the best dancing I've ever seen you do."

"No one's ever gotten a ninety-seven for a dance in the quad city tournament," Ashley said. "So be prepared, girls. We might not take this."

The girls saw one of the judges gather up some papers. The judges were getting ready to make their announcement, and the girls got quiet.

"The Yardley team has earned a . . . ," there was a long pause, "ninety-eight—a record score.

Congratulations to Yardley. You have won the quad city competition!"

Mercy's team screamed and ran around the gym. Not only had they beaten their archrival, they had broken the quad city record for a dance score. As it started to sink in that they were the champions, Mercy walked over to Lydia, Jill, and Kyla.

"I can't believe that we pulled this off," Mercy said. "If it wasn't for all of you, I wouldn't have gotten my balance back!"

"Seeing you work so hard encouraged me to work hard too," Jill said.

"Me too," Kyla said.

"I'm so glad that you didn't give up," Lydia said.

"I'm back in step!" Mercy said, smiling.

As they received their first-place medals, Mercy stood straight, head and shoulders above her teammates, proud to be so tall and graceful.

ABOUT the AUTHOR

Wendy L. Brandes is a lawyer and a teacher. She has written a number of books for children, including Capstone's Summer Camp series. Though she isn't much of a dancer, she loves pop music and watching all different kinds of dance. In her spare time, she enjoys creating crossword puzzles, knitting, and watching her favorite sports teams.

GLOSSARY

appreciation (uh-pree-shee-AY-shuhn)—feeling of being grateful and thankful

assessment (uh-SES-muhnt)—test or evaluation to find out how good or bad something is

concentrate (KON-suhn-trate)—to focus one's thoughts and attention on something

demonstrating (DEM-uhn-strate-ing)—showing other people how to do something

determined (di-TUR-mind)—having reached a firm decision

guaranteed (ga-ruhn-TEED)—made sure of or secure

routine (roo-TEEN)—performance or act that is carefully worked out so it can be repeated

suppressing (suh-PRESS-ing)—stopping something from happening

temporarily (tem-puh-RAIR-uh-lee)—for only a short time

DISCUSSION QUESTIONS

1. Mercy didn't want to go to her coach and ask for help because she was worried about being benched the way Ashley had been during the previous season. Explain how Mercy's and Ashley's situations differed. Do you think Mercy's concern was justified?

2. Was it reasonable for Mercy to expect one private lesson to solve the problems she was having? Why or why not?

3. Do you think that Mercy's parents should have been more involved with helping her work on her problem? How might the story have been different if they had been more involved?

WRITING PROMPTS

1. Dance is considered to be an art form, but it can also be considered a sport. Write an essay to explain how it is like a sport, referencing examples from the book.

2. Would you want to be on a team with Mercy? Using examples from the text, write an essay about how Mercy acts as a teammate.

3. Choose a scene from the book and write a journal entry from the point of view of one of the characters from the book. Be sure to include a description of what happened, as well as an explanation of how the character feels.

LEARN THE TERMS

barre: handrail that is placed on a wall to help people practice dance moves and is often used in ballet

center of gravity: spot in the body that most of a person's weight centers around (for taller people, the center of gravity is higher up and it becomes easier for them to lose their balance or get knocked over)

dance team: group that dances together, often in front of judges (dance teams will dance to different kinds of music, including jazz, ballet, hip-hop, and K-pop)

handspring: gymnastics move where a person lunges forward, rotates his or her body, pushes off the floor, and comes back to a standing position

hip-hop: music that usually goes with rapping

K-pop: South Korean popular music

pirouette: dance turn performed on one foot

sync: to match up and do something at the same time (girls on dance teams often try to sync their steps up to each other)

tango: dance that comes from Africa, South America, Central America, and Europe; during the tango a dancer usually takes small steps and snaps his or her head

vine step: also called a grapevine, this move is a sequence of four repeating steps: side step, step behind the supporting foot, side step, and step in front of the supporting foot

walkover: somersault where someone goes into a handstand and slowly brings the feet backward down to the floor, ending up in a bridge, then springing back to his or her feet